Contents

Contents

BiLLY BONKERS

and the WACKY WORLD CUP!

Giles Andreae
Illustrated by Spike Gerrell

ORCHARD

Giles Andreae is an award-winning
children's author who has written many
bestselling picture books, including
Giraffes Can't Dance and *Commotion in the Ocean*.

He is also the creator of the phenomenally
successful Purple Ronnie, Britain's favourite stick
man. Giles lives by the river near Oxford with his
wife and four young children.

Football Fever!

RRRINNGGG!

The alarm clock juddered across the bedside table and fell off the edge into the bin. Billy Bonkers threw back his duvet, bounced up and down on his bed until the springs twanged, and then sprinted into his parents' room.

"Dad, Mum, wake up!" he bellowed. "It's here! It's time!"

Mr Bonkers sat bolt upright and raised his arms in a silent cheer. His eyes remained shut, however, and Billy suspected that he was still asleep. He took a deep breath.

Mrs Bonkers shrieked and fell out of bed, still wrapped in the duvet cover. Mr Bonkers opened his eyes and leapt to his feet.

"Quick, Billy!" he yelled. "Where are my slippers? Why aren't you dressed yet? What time's kick-off?"

Mrs Bonkers was still flailing around on the floor, and Billy had to step over her to check the match planner on the wall. He had made sure that there was one in every room, so that he would never miss a game.

"Three o'clock in Brazil, which makes it seven o'clock here," Billy replied. "Only twelve hours to go! Hooray!"

Mr Bonkers rubbed his hands together with glee. Mrs Bonkers unwrapped herself from the duvet and heaved herself back onto the bed as if she were climbing Mount Everest.

Billy hurtled back into his own room and started pulling clothes out of his T-shirt drawer. His sister Betty appeared in the doorway, pulling on her dressing gown. "I'm not sure they quite heard you at the end of the street," she said, yawning. "Betty, the World Cup starts today!" cried Billy.

"No kidding!" said Betty, looking around with a grin.

Billy's pyjamas were decorated with a pattern of footballs and the signatures of the whole England squad. The walls of his room were completely hidden by posters of all the players, and there were copies of the match planner on the wardrobe, the ceiling (so that he could read it in bed) and the fish bowl. Billy's goldfish Snapper was a football fan too.

Half an hour later, the Bonkers family were sitting around the kitchen table, scoffing sausages.

"I love the goals best," said Billy. "Bam! Back of the net! That's my favourite bit."

"No way, it's the lead-up to the goals that's the best bit!" said Betty. "The tactics! The teamwork!"

"You're both wrong," said Mr Bonkers, thumping his fist on the table and making the cutlery jump into the air. "It's the WINNING that's the best bit! Nothing else matters!"

"Yes, dear," said Mrs Bonkers, patting her husband on the head. "Now, who wants some porridge?"

"Me," said Billy, chomping through a mouthful of sausages and picking up a bowl of porridge oats. "Mum, what do you like best about football?"

"Ooh," said Mrs Bonkers. "Well, I think the offside rule is lovely. Now, I have a pile of laundry to get through today and your shirt is going in it."

Billy dropped his porridge bowl and clutched his shirt. He had been wearing it for seven days – ever since he bought it with his pocket money. It was an exact replica of the England strip, and Billy's plan was to wear it for the entire World Cup. That wasn't Mrs Bonkers' plan.

"Oh my goodness, you can't wear that

shirt for a month!"
she said.

"But it's a tribute!"
said Billy, holding
onto the shirt
with one hand and
spooning porridge
oats into his mouth with
the other.

"A tribute to what?" asked Betty.
"Stinkiness?"

"I'm going to wear this shirt to watch
every single match," said Billy. "It'll be good
luck for the team!"

"And bad luck for the family," said Betty,
pinching her nose.

Everyone laughed, even Billy. Nothing
could spoil the mood of the Bonkers
family today.

Mr Bonkers checked his watch again.

"Eleven hours, seventeen minutes and, um...twenty-three seconds to go," he said.

Mrs Bonkers sighed. At the same time as the match, on another channel, her favourite Argentine Tango expert would be performing on *Strictly Dancing with Hunks*. She was going to have to miss it. *Never mind*, she thought. *It's only once every four years.*

Usually, her family managed to keep their love of football under control. Mr Bonkers did a bit of complaining when he read the sports pages at breakfast, Betty made predictions about who would end up at the bottom of the league and Billy practised his keepy-uppy skills at the foot of the garden. But for the next month, all they would be able to think about was the World Cup in Brazil. Mr Bonkers had even taken his entire year's allowance of holiday to spend watching the games.

"Not much time to get everything ready," Mr Bonkers was saying. "We'll need snacks, drinks, flags ... Piglet, how many flags do we have?"

"Piglet" was Mr Bonkers's pet name for Mrs Bonkers. She thought it was sweet, and sometimes called him "Sausage" in return.

"There are three on the car, one wrapped around the chimney, two on the shed and one under Billy's bedroom window," said Mrs Bonkers, counting them up on her fingers.

"Madness!" said Mr Bonkers. "Not nearly enough!"

"I could go and get some more, Dad," said Billy.

Mr Bonkers patted him on the head and picked up his newspaper. His eyebrows rocketed to the top of his forehead.

"Listen to this!" he exclaimed, bounding half out of his seat. *"Our roving reporter has scored an inside scoop that'll make the*

*World Cup **WILD**. The England team has been secretly training a brand-new player! He'll be the talk of the terraces, and we don't even know his name. But the whisper is that England's new number seven is*

BETTER THAN BECKHAM!"

Billy wolfed down the rest of his porridge and tried to grab the paper.

"Let me see, Dad!" he pleaded.

"There's no photo," said Mr Bonkers. "Says here that they're keeping him a secret until the last possible minute. Ha! That's the way to scare the opposition! France will be quaking in their studded boots!"

Mr Bonkers had taken a dislike to the French team after their goalkeeper had said that no England player could ever get a goal past him. His greatest World Cup dream, after England winning, was that France would be knocked out in the first round.

Mr Bonkers opened his mouth to explain exactly why France was going to lose, but at that moment the phone rang.

"International number," said Mr Bonkers, looking at the screen. "Who could that be?"

"Maybe it's a wrong number," said Billy.

"Maybe it's an overseas call centre," said Mrs Bonkers.

"Maybe you should answer it and find out," said Betty, handing it to him.

Mr Bonkers stood up and answered the phone. Everyone listened, trying to figure out who it could be.

"Hello?" said Mr Bonkers in a suspicious voice. "Who? Oh! Hello. What? Yes, of course, isn't everyone? Oh. Yes, of course we would, but... WHAT?"

Everyone stared at Mr Bonkers, who was now pacing up and down the kitchen. His eyes were popping out of his head. There was a long silence as he listened to whoever was speaking on the other end of the phone. Then he put his hand on his forehead.

"No problem," he said. "Absolutely no problem. Yes, I've got your address."

Mr Bonkers hung up and held out his arm to Billy.

"Pinch me," he said. "I'm scared I might be dreaming."

Billy gave him a strong pinch, and Mr Bonkers yelled. "Ouch! Not that hard," he said. Then a huge grin spread across his face.

"That was Bruno Bonkeiro, my Brazilian fifth cousin six times removed," he said in a breathless voice. "He lives in Rio, and – can you believe this? – he hates football! He wants to do a house swap with us for the whole World Cup! Piglet, Betty, Billy my son...

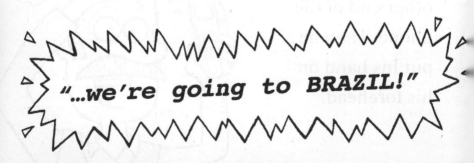

"...we're going to BRAZIL!"

Betty and Billy leapt out of their seats, squealing and whooping. Even Mrs Bonkers gasped in delight.

"Brazil!" said Betty in excitement. "It'll be full of football!"

"Your cousin must be loopy!" said Billy.

Mrs Bonkers was thinking about a magazine article she had read called *The Macho Men of Rio*.

"I shall need a new frock," she said.

They managed to get a flight that night, which meant that they would miss the opening match of the World Cup on TV. But even Billy agreed that it was worth it.

They all left notes for the Bonkeiros. Billy explained how to feed Snapper.

Betty left directions for getting to the library.

Mrs Bonkers wrote instructions for using the washing machine, and Mr Bonkers described how to get past the booby traps that kept his shed secure.

"Lordy lorks, I'm a bag of nerves," said Mrs Bonkers.

They were all in the airport shop, waiting for their flight to be called. Betty was choosing a book for the journey, Billy was trying to think of a way to get into the stadium for the World Cup final and Mr Bonkers was flicking through the sports car magazines. Mrs Bonkers was trying to choose a new perfume, but she couldn't stop thinking about the flight.

You see, **Mrs Bonkers was petrified of flying.**

I expect you know that some people get nervous about flying in an aeroplane. But Mrs Bonkers took it to a whole new level. She broke into a sweat just looking at pictures of aeroplanes. She didn't even feel excited when Mr Bonkers bought Billy a new number seven football T-shirt, so that his old one could be washed.

"ALL PASSENGERS FOR FLIGHT BB304 TO RIO, YOUR FLIGHT IS NOW BOARDING," said a smug voice over the loudspeaker. "PLEASE PROCEED IMMEDIATELY TO GATE NUMBER FOUR, AND DON'T DAWDLE."

Mrs Bonkers took out a flask of tea and a

large yellow tablet. Every time she had to fly, she always took a Super-Duper-Knockout sleeping tablet just before boarding. She dropped the tablet into the tea and waited for it to dissolve. Then she swigged it down. As soon as they were on the plane, she fell fast asleep.

Now, you probably already know that there are two types of flight, short-haul and long-haul. Short-haul flights are quick, and the most you get is a boring magazine and a packet of nuts. That's the sort of flight that the Bonkers family had always been on before. Long-haul flights, on the other hand, offer all sorts of exciting ways to pass the time. There were lots of things that the Bonkers family didn't know about.

Mr Bonkers didn't know about the free newspapers.

Billy didn't know about the free films and the free food.

Betty didn't know about the flight-tracking screen where she could follow their journey on a map.

And nobody knew that Mrs Bonkers' Super-Duper-Knockout sleeping tablet would only work for three quarters of the flight time.

At first, everything went well. Mrs Bonkers was snoring and drooling on the aeroplane blanket. Mr Bonkers was doing a crossword and sulking because Betty kept having to help him. Billy was watching a film and working his way through the flight attendant's collection of meals and snacks.

You or I would think twice before snacking on aeroplane food. After all, it's even more disgusting than school dinners when Mr Bonkers was a boy, and that's saying something. But Billy had unusual tastes. He liked dry porridge oats. He liked rock-hard pork pies. And he absolutely LOVED aeroplane food.

Anyway, everyone was enjoying the flight in their own way when suddenly Mrs Bonkers gave a loud, snuffling snort and opened her eyes.

"PANIC STATIONS!"

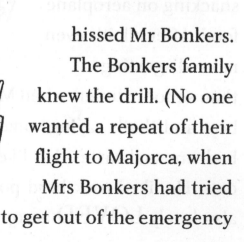

hissed Mr Bonkers. The Bonkers family knew the drill. (No one wanted a repeat of their flight to Majorca, when Mrs Bonkers had tried to get out of the emergency exit halfway there, and had to be sat on by a large flight attendant until the flight landed.) Mr Bonkers pulled down the blind so she couldn't see that they were above the clouds. Betty snapped a pink eye mask with fluffy edging over her eyes. Billy grabbed the flask and the box of sleeping tablets, and darted up to the front of the plane to get some more tea.

The flight attendants had already become very familiar with Billy's appetite. They had never before had to carry so many trays of food to one passenger, and they were feeling very tired. So they had told Billy that he could help himself to whatever he wanted. They didn't bat an eyelid when they saw him filling a flask with tea.

Billy dropped the last Super-Duper-Knockout sleeping tablet into the flask. Then he put it down and turned around to get himself just one more little packet of biscuits.

That was Billy's big mistake.

It just so happened that on flight BB304 there

was a new flight attendant called Mabel. Mabel wasn't exactly brilliant at her job, but she was determined to make a good impression. And she knew that the Captain liked to have a flask of tea shortly before landing.

Have you ever noticed that disasters have a way of starting from something as small and meaningless as, for example, a flask of tea?

While Billy's back was turned, Mabel picked up the flask and carried it through to the cockpit. The Captain, who was feeling very thirsty, thanked her and shared it with the co-pilot.

Meanwhile, Billy was hunting high and low for the flask.

"Excuse me," he said as Mabel hurried past. "Have you seen a red flask full of tea?"

"I certainly have, little boy," said Mabel. "Don't worry, I've already given it to the Captain. Now, run along back to your seat, sweetie-pie. It won't be long before we land."

She put her hands on his shoulders and steered him back to his seat. I don't know about you, but Billy found her really quite annoying. He could just about cope with "little boy", but "sweetie-pie" was more than anyone should have to endure. He slumped into his seat and Betty looked at him in alarm.

"Where's the flask?" she demanded.

"That," said Billy, "is the question."

He explained what had happened, and Betty rolled her eyes.

"It's OK," she said. "The co-pilot can land the plane, and we'll just have to make another flask of tea for Mum. Simple!"

"Except that I used the last sleeping tablet," said Billy.

"Hmm, that complicates things," said Betty.

She glanced over at Mrs Bonkers, who

gave a big yawn. Mr Bonkers gave them a desperate look. As soon as Mrs Bonkers woke up properly and realised that she was still in the air, there would be pandemonium.

"We're going to need a very large flight

attendant," he said.

"Wait a minute," said Betty. "I think I might have an idea!"

She grabbed Mr Bonkers' newspaper and turned to the sports section.

"Quick," she said. "Read every single football article out loud."

"Have you gone mad?" asked Mr Bonkers. "That'll excite her!"

"It will excite you, Dad," said Betty, "but Mum can't stand all that football talk. 'Boring, unreconstructed, time-wasting man-drivel', she calls it, remember?"

"Oh, um, yes, I remember," said Mr Bonkers sheepishly, and he started to read.

Mrs Bonkers began snoring almost immediately.

"Come on," said Betty. "Let's go and get that flask back. We'll just have to explain to the Captain that it was an accident, and not your fault."

Luckily, there were no flight attendants around to stop them reaching the cockpit. Mabel (who was really not at all good at her job) had left the cockpit door open, and Betty and Billy slipped inside and closed it behind them.

"Oh dear," said Billy, which was an understatement.

He suddenly understood the phrase "hot under the collar". The Captain was fast asleep in his seat, with his head tipped back and his legs and arms splayed out.

Unfortunately, so was the co-pilot.

Billy started feeling very hot under the collar indeed.

"They must have shared the tea!" said Betty with a groan. "We have to get help."

"Wait!" cried Billy, grabbing his sister's arm.

He pointed to a notice on the cockpit door.

> ## ANY PERSON OR PERSONS WHO DISTURB, DISTRACT OR DISCOMBOBULATE THE CAPTAIN WILL BE ARRESTED. <u>NO EXCEPTIONS</u>!

Betty gazed at the notice for a moment. Then she turned to Billy with a determined look on her face. Billy knew that look, and it made him feel very nervous.

"We can't tell anyone or we'll be arrested as soon as we land," she said. "We've disturbed, distracted AND discombobulated the Captain. There's only one thing for it. We'll have to land the plane ourselves."

"Are you joking?" said Billy. "We're just kids! How can we land a massive plane full of people?"

"There's an instruction manual here," said Betty, picking up a booklet from the side. "Besides,  you're always playing that flying game on your console. How hard can it be?"

Billy gawped at her, but he didn't say anything.

Have you ever stood at a crossroads, not knowing which way to go? Well, Billy's brain had arrived at a crossroads...and it didn't have a clue.

On the one hand, he thought it was possible that his sister had gone completely stark, staring, loop-the-loop mad.

On the other hand, this was a once-in-alifetime never-to-be-repeated opportunity to really, actually fly a real, actual plane.

Do you know what you would have done? Well, Billy took a deep breath.

"OK," he said. "I suppose we've got no choice. You read, I'll fly."

Together, Billy and Betty propped the Captain and co-pilot up against the side of the cockpit. Then Billy sat down and looked at the dials, levers and switches in front of him. There were millions of them! Luckily, there was a comforting green light next to the word "Autopilot". It did look amazingly similar to his computer game.

"Are you ready, Billy?" Betty asked, opening the instruction manual.

Billy took another deep breath.

"Ready!" he said, turning off the autopilot button.

"First, level the aircraft," said Betty.

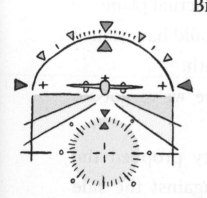

Billy took hold of the control yoke and looked at the artificial horizon on the screen. The miniature wings were steady. Perfect. "So far, so good," he said.

"Maintain a safe speed," read Betty.

Billy checked the airspeed indicator. The needle was wavering around safely in a green zone.

"Wicked!" he said under his breath. "I'm flying! I'm actually flying!"

Just then, the radio crackled.

"This is flight control," said a voice. **"Welcome to Rio! Please use runway number three. You're on target, so you can just fly straight in."**

Billy found the microphone and pressed the button to speak.

"Roger, flight control," he said.

"Are you all right?" asked the flight controller, sounding surprised. **"Your voice is very squeaky."**

"Just a bit of a cold," growled Billy. "Over and out."

Betty pressed a button on the wall.

"That tells the flight attendants to prepare to land," she said. "This is it! Er... Billy, just out of interest, how many times have you landed a plane safely in your computer game?"

Billy stared straight ahead and tightened his grip on the yoke.

"Just keep reading the instructions," he said firmly.

Betty sat down in the co-pilot's seat and fastened her seatbelt. Billy could see the runway below.

"You have to reduce power," said Betty, leafing through the pages of the manual. "Pull back the throttle, and stop when the sound of the engines changes."

By pulling back on the throttle, Billy made the nose of the aeroplane drop. They were coming in to land!

"Lower the landing gear using the gear handle on your right," Betty read aloud. "Then activate reverse thrust."

Billy followed her instructions and the plane dropped lower. The ground was rushing up to meet them! His heart thumped as he pulled the throttle all the way towards him.

"Woohoo!" yelled Billy as the wheels hit the tarmac.

"BRAKE!"

squealed Betty.

Billy pressed the pedals and the plane slowed to a stop.

"Oh cripes," said a voice behind them. "We've landed!"

It was the Captain! He shook the co-pilot awake and they both gawped at Billy.

"What on Earth are you doing here?" they gasped in unison.

"Um, well, errr..." stammered Billy. He was really in trouble now.

"He only went and landed the plane," said Betty proudly. "Your plane!"

"This is what comes of staying up late to talk about football," said the Captain with a groan. Then he looked at Billy. "Well, if it hadn't been for you, I don't know what would have happened. You're a hero, boy. A HERO!"

"I guess I just did what I had to," said Billy, trying to look modest. "I'm no one special."

But the Captain didn't agree. He took a

wing-shaped gold badge from his shoulder and handed it to Billy.

"This is for you," he said. "Only experienced pilots are allowed to wear it, and I think you deserve it. You saved the day!"

"Wow!" said Billy. "Thanks, Captain!"

"And, er, could you please not mention this little incident to anyone?" the Captain added. "I could get into big trouble."

"Your secret's safe with us," said Billy with a grin. "Besides, I've got more important things to think about. If I can land a plane, I must be able to think of a way to see the World Cup final. Rio, here we come!"

Final Frenzy!

"YES! YES! YES!" screamed Mr Bonkers, hurling his baseball cap into the sky.

"WOOHOO!" shouted Betty, jumping up and down.

Billy leapt into the air with his arms raised up in a silent cheer. He had lost his voice from shouting about three-quarters of the way through the match, but he didn't care. Nothing mattered except the amazing, stupendous, earth-shatteringly fantastic news that ENGLAND WERE THROUGH TO THE WORLD CUP FINAL!

The big square in the middle of Rio was packed with football fans. There were tall fans and short fans. There were skinny fans and plump fans. There were people from all sorts of different countries and homes, but they all had one thing in common. Football!

Together, they had been watching the match on a huge open-air screen. Flags, football scarves and clackers were flying in all directions, and everyone seemed to want to hug everyone else.

"Nail-biting!" Mr Bonkers was bellowing, his sunglasses wonky due to a kiss from a rather excitable Brazilian lady. "Never seen a semi-final like it! Incredible! They're GODS!"

"But are they good enough to beat France?" asked Betty.

Billy bit his fingernails. (This is, of course, a very unpleasant habit. As a matter of fact, Billy had never done it before, but the situation called for it.)

"They have to!" he croaked.

"Beat France?" Mr Bonkers shouted.

He tried to run his fingers through the thin hair on top of his head.

"Can England beat France?" he repeated. "Do ducks like the rain? Do bears poo in the woods? Does your mother make the best pork pies in the world? Of COURSE they can beat France!"

He took a handkerchief from his pocket and mopped his brow.

"Isn't this amazing?" said Betty, looking around at the crowds that surrounded them. "I've heard people speaking Spanish and German and Chinese and loads of other languages that I don't even recognise."

Mr Bonkers stopped bouncing and suddenly looked very serious. He held up his hand with one finger raised. Billy and

Betty looked at each other in dismay. They knew exactly what this meant. Mr Bonkers was about to make a speech.

Mr Bonkers liked making speeches, but he hardly ever got the chance. Usually, Mrs Bonkers suddenly remembered something important she had to do in another room, while Billy and Betty made a dash for it. But now there was nowhere to run. They were surrounded by hordes of celebrating football fans.

"Don't need to speak the same language when you all love football," Mr Bonkers proclaimed. "One kick of the ball and you're best friends for life! Football – international language! Builds friendships, keeps you fit."

Billy and Betty had stopped listening. Betty was busy calculating the exact odds of England winning the World Cup. And Billy was desperately trying to think of a way to get a ticket for the final. Now that England was through, he had to see the final, no matter what. He just had to!

Rio was full of football, and it had made Billy's football fever even worse. Billy, Betty and Mr Bonkers had spent every day since they had arrived watching matches or repeats of matches on the big screens that had been set up around the city while Mrs Bonkers had gone sightseeing with her *Hunk Spotter's Guide to Rio* tucked under her arm. They had hardly been in the house except to sleep.

Absentmindedly, Billy pulled his fifth pork pie of the afternoon out of his bag and munched on it. He sat down on his bag and rubbed his legs. They were feeling a bit like cooked spaghetti after all the jumping up and down.

In just two days England would play France in the World Cup final. There had to be some way that he could get to see the match. He just needed to have the time to think about it without interruptions.

"...and that's how football could bring about world peace," concluded Mr Bonkers. "Well, I've got to go and find your mother. I promised her that I'd meet her after the match to do some sightseeing.

You two know your way back to the house, don't you?"

Billy and Betty nodded and waved goodbye as Mr Bonkers elbowed his way through the crowd.

Billy swallowed the last of his pork pie and took a long swig of water.

"That's better," he said in a hoarse whisper.

It took them a long time to walk back to the house. There were parties on every street corner. An English family danced across the road. A group of pretty German girls were dancing outside a café, and they grabbed Billy and Betty and made them dance too.

The whole of Rio seemed to be celebrating, and the Bonkers family were celebrating with them.

They were walking up the quiet, narrow street towards their house when Billy saw something that stopped him in his tracks.

"What is it?" asked Betty, sidestepping him. "You look like your goldfish."

It was true that Billy's mouth was hanging open, but there was a very good reason for that. Outside a small, dirty-looking shop was a large billboard. It was wobbling in the wind, and it looked as if someone had written on it in thick red marker pen:

EXTRA FINAL TICKETS AVAILABLE HERE!

Billy's heart was thumping like an enormous drum. Blood rushed to his head and made him feel hot and dizzy. He thought he heard distant music, and he felt a wave of love for the whole world, even the French football team.

"Dreams do come true!" he whispered.

Betty's voice scratched through his thoughts.

"Oh no they don't, Billy," she said. "Not that one, anyway. It can't be true. All the tickets were sold ages ago, and besides, it would cost a bomb. Come on."

She pulled Billy along the street and into their house. Billy was still reeling from the idea that there might be some tickets for the final just a few doors away.

He thought about the tickets all through dinner. He put vinegar on his bread rolls,

butter on his sausages
and chocolate milk on his
chips, and he didn't even
notice.

"Are you feeling all right,
Billy dear?" asked Mrs Bonkers.

She put her hand on his forehead and
gazed at him.

"I'm fine, Mum," said Billy. "But I'm just
going to EXPLODE if I can't be there for
the final."

"But can't you just watch it on a
big screen, like all the others?" asked
Mrs Bonkers.

"Yes," said Betty, snaffling one of Billy's
sausages. "Yes, he can."

Billy gave a long, loud sigh.

"It's not the same, Mum," he said. "I've
got to BE there."

Before he went to bed, Billy hung up his England shirt on the wardrobe door. Then he climbed into bed and gazed at it.

"There's got to be a way," he said with a yawn...

William Benedict Bertwhistle Bonkers is dreaming.

It's the last minute of the World Cup final and Billy's team needs one more goal to win. But they can't get past the defence! Suddenly the captain spots Billy leaning over the side. "It's Billy Bonkers!" he yells. "Help us, Billy!"

Billy leaps over the side and races onto the

pitch. He gets the ball and ducks and weaves around the other team. He's just a blur! The crowd goes wild as Billy zooms towards the goal. Nothing can stop this amazing boy! He shoots. He scores! He—

Brrrriiiing! Brrrriiiiing! Brrrrriiiiing!

Billy woke up and gave a sigh. The alarm clock was going off, but he hadn't reached his favourite part of the dream yet, where the team hoisted him on their shoulders and the crowd chanted his name.

That dream was the thing that made up Billy's mind.

Now, if you are anything like Mrs Bonkers, you won't know why actually being at the match was so important. But if you are like Billy, you will understand that this might be his only chance to be at a World Cup final with England playing. You will understand that the very thought of being there made his heart hammer and his palms go sweaty. You will understand that watching a match on a screen couldn't compare to being in the stadium with the players, surrounded by thousands of singing, cheering fans.

Billy threw off his bedcovers and pulled on his shorts and England top. Then he picked up the small tin where he kept all his holiday spending money, slipped it into his pocket and tiptoed out of the house. There was already a queue outside the shop, and Billy joined it. There were only five people ahead of him, so he hoped that he would be lucky. He crossed his fingers and waited.

One by one the people in front of him disappeared into the funny little shop. When they came out again, they all hurried away without looking back. Billy gulped. Did that mean that they had got tickets or not?

The man in front of Billy had just gone into the shop when Betty came sprinting down the street.

"I guessed you were here," she puffed when she reached his side. "You missed breakfast! There's only one thing in the world that could make you do that."

"Football!" said Billy, grinning at her.

But Betty didn't smile back. She put one hand on her hip and held up the other one, counting each thing she said off on her fingers.

"Billy, this is a really, really bad idea," she said. "No one has tickets to the final! These tickets are probably fakes. If they're not fakes, they're stolen. Besides, they'll be way too expensive for you. Stop being silly and come home now, before Mum and Dad find out."

Has anyone ever ordered you to do something in a very bossy voice? It's a funny thing, but suddenly you find that you want to do the exact opposite. That's just how Billy felt when Betty narrowed her eyes, folded her arms and told him to come back to the house. Up until that moment he had been feeling quite nervous about spending all his holiday money. But when Betty told him that it was a silly thing to do, he made up his mind.

"You can't order me around," he said.

"It's my money, and I want a ticket to the final!"

The man in front of him came out of the shop and darted away down the street. Billy took a deep  breath, squeezed the tin in his pocket and then marched into the shop.

It was very gloomy inside, and the walls were bare. A small man with black hair was sitting at a rickety old desk. There was an ice-cream tub full of money beside him.

"Um, one ticket please," said Billy, opening his tin and taking out his money. "Er, how much will that be?"

The man's eyes narrowed as he gazed at the money.

"All," he said, holding out his hand.

At that precise moment Billy heard two voices in his head.

"This is a spectacularly bad idea," said the first voice. "It'll go down in history as one of the worst ideas ever."

"You will never get this chance again," said the second voice. "Do it!"

The first voice sounded a bit like Betty. Billy plonked the money down on the desk.

The man gave a grin that showed he was missing most of his front teeth. He scooped the money into the ice-cream tub. Then he opened a drawer and pulled out a single ticket, embossed in shining silver.

Billy heard trumpets and fanfares. He heard the distant sound of an enormous imaginary cheer. As he took the  ticket and staggered out into the sunlight, he felt dizzy with happiness. Forgetting about his argument with Betty, he ran up to her, waving the ticket.

"I got one!" he yelled. "I got one!"

Betty snatched the ticket out of his hand. She pulled a face that looked amazingly like Mrs Bonkers.

"Billy, I can't believe you did that!" she said. "What will Mum and Dad say?"

"Dad will say 'Well done' and 'Go and get me one'!" Billy exclaimed, feeling dizzy with excitement. "Woohoo! I'm going to the final!"

Betty made an exasperated noise through her nostrils. I don't exactly know how to write it, but it sounded a bit like a cross horse and a bit like the air being let out of a balloon. It was something like:

PHOOOOSHHHHUMPH!

At that moment, there was a sudden and very WHOOSHY gust of wind. It plucked the ticket from between her fingers and sent it fluttering down the street.

"No!" Billy shouted.

"Come back!"

He plunged down the street after the ticket, with Betty sprinting behind him.

The wind took the ticket swirling to the road at the bottom of the street, where it danced across car bonnets to the opposite side.

BEEEEEEEEP!

Car horns hooted as Billy dived across the road.

"Billy, STOP!" Betty cried.

Billy wasn't listening. That ticket was his only chance of seeing the World Cup Final. There was no way he was letting it out of his sight!

The ticket drifted to the ground by the entrance to a busy market. Billy threw himself along the pavement towards it. His fingertips were millimetres away when a group of shoppers hurried past, creating a draught that whisked the ticket up into the market.

Billy gave a cry of despair, pulled himself to his feet

and raced into the crowd, his eyes fixed on the little white rectangle of paper. Shoppers threw themselves aside as he charged towards them, head down and legs pumping.

"Stop that ticket!" he yelled.

The ticket whirled around the shoppers'

feet, now attached to the sole of a red high heel, now clinging to the side of a muddy trainer. Every time Billy got close, it was sent fluttering away from him. Close to the exit on the opposite side of the market, another breeze scooped up the ticket and carried it over the heads of the shoppers and out into the street. Billy clambered over bags and shopping trolleys, keeping his eyes fixed on

the ticket. It was high above his head now, circling as if wondering which direction to take. Billy watched and waited.

Have you ever seen a bird of prey diving on a small mouse from a great height? Perhaps you have seen someone drop a large boulder from a high bridge?

Well, Billy's ticket moved faster than either of those two things. Without warning, it dropped out of the sky, swooped into the open window of a red car and landed on the back seat.
As if it had been
waiting or it, the
engine roared
into life and
the car pulled
away from
the kerb.

"NOOOO!" cried Billy.

He grabbed a skateboard from a little

boy who was standing on the street corner.

"I'll bring it back!" he yelled.

Unfortunately, the little boy didn't speak English. He shouted a few rather rude words in Portuguese, and then went to look

for a policeman. (He would have a lot of explaining to do if he went home without it, because it belonged to his older brother, who didn't know he had borrowed it.)

Meanwhile, Billy was scooting through the crazy Rio traffic after the car. Luckily, everything was happening too fast for him to think about it. I say "luckily", because

Billy had never actually ridden a skateboard in real life before.

"Virtual skateboarding is definitely not the same thing," he said to himself as he 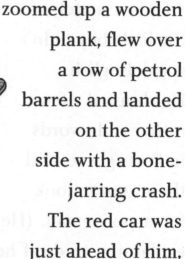 zoomed up a wooden plank, flew over a row of petrol barrels and landed on the other side with a bone-jarring crash. The red car was just ahead of him, caught up in a traffic jam. *Closer! Closer!* But just as his hand touched the door, the car pulled away and turned down a side street.

Billy sliced sideways, ducked under a parked lorry and sped between two sports

cars. The drivers swerved and crashed into two metal bollards with loud crunching noises. Unfortunately for Billy, one of them was a police car.

Unaware of the shouts, yells and radio reports behind him, Billy stood sideways on the skateboard and hurtled down a steep hill after the red car. He was gathering speed now. Then, to his horror, he suddenly realised that the red car was slowing down to turn left.

"Where are the brakes?!" he hollered as he hurtled past an elderly lady at forty miles an hour.

The elderly lady threw her shopping into the air in shock, and five fresh tomatoes splatted onto her head.

As the red car turned, Billy managed to grab the back bumper. He was swung around to the left, the skateboard wheels juddering over the bumpy ground.

"I d-d-d-don't r-r-r-really l-l-l-like th-this ver-ver-ver-very much!" he howled.

He lost his grip on the bumper, but he was still rocketing along at almost the same speed as the car.

Behind him, the policeman whose car had just crashed had grabbed a passer-by's bicycle and was now in hot pursuit, directing other units on his police radio.

Billy passed a series of signs pointing down the hill. They were mostly just blurs, but one of them showed a picture of some wavy lines. Billy groaned, because he knew that sign meant water. He was speeding down a steep hill towards the docks, and he had absolutely no braking system.

The sound of police sirens behind him was getting louder, but he hardly noticed. The red car was right in front of him. All he had to do was to find a way to stop it. He scooted through a tower of cardboard boxes that were piled up at the side of the road.

He shot past a street seller with a vegetable cart, and had to shake three courgettes out of his T-shirt. Nothing could stop this boy! The hill seemed to get a little less steep, and Billy finally felt himself slowing down. The red car was slowing too. It came to a halt at the edge of the dock, and Billy aimed for a raised wooden flowerbed nearby. The skateboard hit the wooden edge and catapulted Billy headfirst into the flowers.

Spitting petals out of his mouth, Billy slid sideways out of the flowerbed, picked up the skateboard and staggered towards the car. He was tomato-red in the face and he didn't think he would ever be able to breathe properly again, but he had done it.

He had found his precious ticket.

Billy was five steps away from the car when a woman jumped out and opened the back door.

"NOOOOO!"

cried Billy.
It was too
late. A salty
gust of sea
air lifted the
ticket out
of the car
and gently
floated it down
to the water.

Billy flung the skateboard aside and took a running dive into the sea, just as five police cars screeched to a halt behind him.

I don't expect that you have ever dived into the water of a working dock. It isn't a very nice place for a swim. There are things floating in there that I probably shouldn't describe, especially if you've just had your tea.

Billy thrashed around in the sea, gasping and trying not to swallow anything. Then he saw it, floating just beside his left shoulder. His ticket! Billy clutched at it...and the paper went to pieces in his hands.

"**NOOOOO!**" he cried for the third time that day.

He looked up and saw a small boat moored nearby. It was packed solid with men, and

they all looked absolutely petrified. In fact, now Billy came to think about it, one of them looked very like the man who sold him the ticket. They were pointing at the police cars and shouting at each other.

"Hey!" yelled Billy. "Help!"

The man who Billy thought he recognised pointed at Billy and started yelling even louder. Then they heaved a couple of suitcases over the side of the boat, started the engine and sped off. The suitcases splashed into the water next to Billy and burst open. He saw a ticket for the final float out. Two... three...four tickets! The words "World Cup Final" swam blurrily in front  of his eyes. The suitcases were filled with hundreds...thousands of tickets.

Billy watched as a police speedboat appeared in the distance, cutting off the men's escape. Then he felt a strong pair of hands on his shoulders and he was pulled into a boat. A policeman wrapped a towel around his shoulders and shook him firmly by the hand.

"Are you English?" he asked.

Billy nodded, his teeth chattering.

"You're a marvel!" said the policeman. "You've done it!"

"D-d-d-d-done w-w-w-what?" said Billy, wondering what on earth he was talking about.

He climbed out of the boat onto the side of the dock and was soon surrounded by policemen who wanted to shake him by the hand. Then he saw Betty glaring at him with her arms folded.

"H-how did you f-find me?" he asked.

"I just followed the trail of damage you left," said his sister, shaking her head. "I hope you've learnt your lesson."

She still sounded scarily like Mrs Bonkers in a bad mood.

"This boy is a hero!" said another policeman, ruffling Billy's hair and grinning at Betty.

"What do you mean?" Betty asked.

"He led us straight to a gang of con artists," the policeman explained. "They've been selling fake football tickets to stupid tourists, and we haven't been able to catch them. Now we've got them all!"

"Stupid tourists?" Betty repeated.

"Well, you'd have to be pretty stupid to believe you could buy a ticket for the final at this stage," said the policeman.

"Yes," said Betty in a thoughtful voice. "Yes, you would."

Billy cleared his throat and edged away, grabbing the skateboard as he went.

"Come on, Betty," he said. "I've got to return this."

"And then what?" asked Betty.

Billy grinned at her. "Then I've just got to think of another way of getting to the final!"

England's Secret Weapon!

"Well folks, it's the day of the World Cup Final 2014, and Rio is poised for its most exciting game ever! Everyone is talking about England's new player. Who

is this secret weapon we've heard so much about? People have already started arriving for the big match, and here at the stadium the atmosphere is promising to be—"

Billy turned off the radio and gave a deep sigh. Everyone was talking about the match, and about England's mysterious secret player – number seven.

Billy had hung around outside the stadium, hoping to meet someone who was trying to sell a ticket. He had even offered to work at the stadium for free, but it was no use. He still didn't have a ticket, and he had run out of ideas. It was fantastic to be in Rio. It was amazing to be in the same city as the World Cup final. But it would be torture if he couldn't actually watch the game!

Billy was sitting at the breakfast table, hunched over his second bowl of dry porridge oats. (You probably know by now that this was Billy's favourite breakfast cereal. Most people add milk to make their porridge soft and mushy, but not Billy Bonkers.)

"Eat up your breakfast, Billy dear," said Mrs Bonkers. "It's a big day today, and I don't want you to faint from hunger. You've only had six sausages and a bowl of porridge. I'm feeling quite worried about you."

She shoved some dirty laundry into the washing machine and pressed the button.

The machine made a loud beeping noise and then let out a squelchy raspberry. Mrs Bonkers gasped.

During the World Cup, they were staying in the home of Bruno Bonkeiro, Mr Bonkers' fifth cousin six times removed. Mrs Bonkers had never been to Brazil before, and she definitely didn't speak the same language as the washing machine.

"Lordy lorks, not again!" she exclaimed. "Nigel! Where are you, Sausage dear?"

Betty looked up from her book for a moment.

"Dad's in the shed," she said.

Ever since England got through to the final, Mr Bonkers had been doing a lot of mysterious banging and thumping in his cousin's garden shed. He had found several interesting bits and bobs in there,

and he had decided that Bruno Bonkeiro
and he had a lot in common.

As Mrs Bonkers
was frowning
at the washing
machine, the back
door burst open
and Mr Bonkers
sprang into the
kitchen. He had
dabs of oil all
over his face and
his hair was thick
with grease, but he looked very, very happy.
Mrs Bonkers started to speak.

"Sausage, the washing machine has—"

"Never mind that now!" cried Mr Bonkers,
waving a spanner above his head like a
flag. "I've done it!"

"Done what?" asked Billy.

Even though he was feeling down in the dumps, he always enjoyed hearing about his dad's experiments. There was usually a risk that something might blow up, which Billy thought added an extra whiff of excitement.

"I've built a machine that will make sure we have the best seats in the house for the final!" Mr Bonkers declared.

Billy sat up very straight and stared at Mr Bonkers.

"Do you mean watching it on a screen from a really good spot?" he asked.

"No, Billy my boy!" shouted Mr Bonkers in glee. "I mean actually being in the stadium!"

Billy let out a yell of delight and jumped up to dance around the table. Betty

whooped and hugged Mr Bonkers. But Mrs Bonkers frowned.

"That sounds lovely, Sausage, but what exactly is this machine?"

"Come and see!" said Mr Bonkers.

He led them all into the garden, and pointed to his creation proudly. Billy fell silent with admiration. Betty gasped in wonder.

A large wicker basket was standing in the middle of the lawn under an enormous patchwork balloon. There was a fireworks rocket attached to each corner of the basket, facing downwards. An old motorbike engine was strapped to the side with bailer twine. Coloured wires ran from the engine to a small portable heater in the middle.

"I call it the Bonkers Electric Rocket-Powered Hot-Air Balloon," said Mr Bonkers. "We can hover right over the game and see everything, because I've made the base of the basket out of see-through plastic!"

"Brilliant, Dad," said Billy in an awed voice.

"Oh my goodness, Sausage," said Mrs Bonkers. "It's very clever, but are you sure it will hold you all up?"

"It's as safe as houses, Piglet," said Mr Bonkers, giving her a reassuring pat on the shoulder. "Nothing can possibly go wrong."

(These, as I am sure you have realised, are what we call "famous last words".)

"Perhaps you should take it for a short test flight around the garden," said Mrs Bonkers.

She knew all about famous last words, because she had been married to Mr Bonkers for a very long time.

"No need, no need," said Mr Bonkers, waving his spanner around again. "I know exactly what I'm doing."

"Well, I'll just go and pack you a few things for the journey," said Mrs Bonkers.

She hurried inside. Billy smoothed down his number seven T-shirt and felt a grin spread across his face. He was going to the final!

"Perhaps I could manage a few more sausages after all," he said.

Ten minutes before the game was due to start, Billy, Betty and

Mr Bonkers clambered into the wicker basket. Mrs Bonkers peered over the side.

"I've put a few things together for you," she said.

She handed them:

Three packed lunches   One inflatable dinghy

One first-aid kit   Three parachutes

One lifebelt   One change of

Three life jackets   underwear per

One torch   person

Squeezed into the tiny remaining space in the basket, Mr Bonkers turned up the portable heater to maximum. He lit the rockets and they started to fizzle and spurt. He untied the ropes that were holding the balloon down.

"Have fun!" called Mrs Bonkers, looking more than a little bit worried. "And remember, Sausage, safety first please. Above everything else...SAFETY."

"BLAST OFF!"

shouted Mr Bonkers.

The rockets sent them shooting high up above the city.

Billy peered over the edge of the basket, while Betty looked through the see-through floor. The streets of Rio were laid out like a living map. The rockets exploded in red,

green and blue sparkles, and then Mr Bonkers licked his finger and held it up. "Just as I thought," he said. "The wind is in exactly the right direction. It'll blow us straight to the stadium!"

At first Mr Bonkers' plan worked brilliantly. The balloon floated to the stadium, where the game had already started. The watching crowds looked like a sea of waving flags, enormous foam hands and crazy hats. Mr Bonkers rummaged around and pulled out a large office fan.

He attached it to the engine and pointed it in the opposite direction to the wind.

"As long as the fan blows at the same strength as the wind, we'll keep hovering over the game," he explained.

Billy grinned up at his dad. He felt very happy that Mr Bonkers was so good at inventions. It was true that some of them didn't always go to plan, but this one was working perfectly.

This is going to be Dad's biggest success, thought Billy.

(These were also famous last words.)

Everyone was too interested in the match to look up, and Billy, Betty and Mr Bonkers had a wonderful bird's-eye view of the game. They shouted encouraging things to the team. They gasped when England got an early chance at a goal. They groaned when the French goalkeeper saved the ball. They yelled advice to the referee at the tops of their voices.

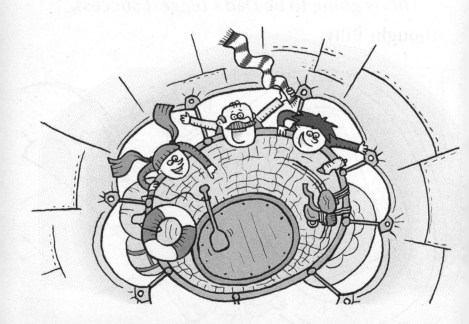

The match was more than halfway through and the score was 2-2 when the engine made a strange noise. It was somewhere between a cough and a hiccup. Billy, Betty and Mr Bonkers slowly turned

their heads to look at each other. Then there was a crackling, spitting sound.

"Blast, blast, BLAST!" groaned Mr Bonkers. "That must be the fuel. I was in such a hurry to get us here on time that I topped up the tank with a bit of oil from your sausage pan, Billy. Didn't think it would make much difference," he added sheepishly.

"Erm, time for those parachutes?" said Betty.

They grabbed the parachutes and pulled them on. Just in the nick of time! The basket gave a tremendous jerk and lurched sideways. Their cargo was strapped in, but Billy, Betty and Mr Bonkers shot out of the basket and went hurtling downwards.

"Pull the cord!" bawled Mr Bonkers.

Billy saw his dad's parachute fly out, followed by Betty's a few seconds later. They floated down safely towards the stands.

Eagerly, he tugged on his own cord. But instead of the whoosh of a parachute, Billy heard a hissing noise and felt something squeezing his body. He had put on the life jacket by mistake!

The life jacket inflated like an enormous yellow tyre. As it swelled up around Billy, he spotted the words "EXTRA LARGE" growing in front of his eyes. The life jacket was so enormous that it turned him into a giant inflated ball. He felt himself hit the ground and bounce.

BOING!

"This is awesome!"
shouted Billy as he
bounced into the air
again.

BOING!

"It's like the best
fairground ride
EVER!" he cried as
he somersaulted
up once more.

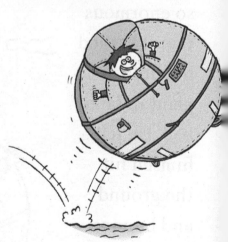

BOING!

Suddenly everything stopped spinning.

Billy looked up and saw a huge, hairy face scowling down at him.

Either he had landed in the gorilla enclosure at the local zoo, or he had bounced into the arms of a very cross security guard.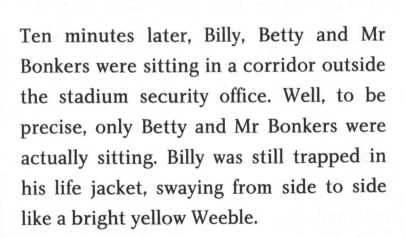

Ten minutes later, Billy, Betty and Mr Bonkers were sitting in a corridor outside the stadium security office. Well, to be precise, only Betty and Mr Bonkers were actually sitting. Billy was still trapped in his life jacket, swaying from side to side like a bright yellow Weeble.

They were waiting for the chief security officer to tell them what he thought

of people who parachuted (or bounced) into the stadium without tickets. Mr Bonkers was in a surprisingly good mood.

"Not a bad result," he kept saying. "Worked for quite a while! And we're IN THE STADIUM! That's an experience worth having."

Billy wanted to remark that he would rather be in the part of the stadium where they could actually see the match being played, but the life jacket was rather tight and made it difficult to speak.

Suddenly, they heard a crackle. The gorilla-like security guard, who had been ordered to watch them, picked up his radio.

"All spare security guards to the west entrance!" ordered a tinny voice. "Three boys and a labradoodle are trying to sneak in. Go get 'em!"

The security guard looked at his prisoners. Billy could guess what he was thinking. Betty and Mr Bonkers had been tied to their seats with their parachute straps, and Billy was a plump boy in a massive yellow inflatable. They weren't going anywhere.

"On my way," the security guard barked into the radio.

With a final glare at Billy, he stamped off down the corridor.

As soon as the guard was out of sight, Betty leaned over and tugged on a cord on Billy's life jacket. It instantly deflated, and Billy stepped out of it, taking deep breaths.

"Thanks, Betty!" he said.

He tried to untie her, but the security guard had made the knots too tight.

"Never mind," said Betty. "Go home and fetch Mum. She'll have to explain and get them to let us go."

"NONSENSE!" shouted Mr Bonkers.

Betty and Billy looked at him in surprise.

"Hokum!" said Mr Bonkers. "Piffle, balderdash and bunk!"

If his arms hadn't been tied to his sides with parachute straps, he would have been waving them in the air.

"England is playing in the World Cup final!" he exclaimed. "Billy, forget about us. Get out into the stadium and watch the end of the match. At least we will be able to say that one Bonkers watched England win the World Cup!"

"But Dad!" cried Betty.

"GO, Billy!" shouted Mr Bonkers.

Billy didn't wait to be told again. He sprinted down the corridor in the opposite direction from the security guard, zoomed around a corner, turned left, turned right... and realised that he was completely lost.

"Oh no!" he cried. "Help!"

But there was no one around. He dashed down corridor after corridor. He went down three flights of stairs and stumbled into five different broom cupboards. He could hear the screams and cheers of the stadium crowd, but he just couldn't work out where they were coming from.

Just as Billy was wondering if he would be stuck in the stadium corridors forever, he heard heavy footsteps coming his way.

His heart thumping, he darted around a corner and dashed into the first room he saw. Billy closed the door and listened. The footsteps went past, and he breathed a sigh of relief. Then he heard a surprised voice behind him.

"Hello! Who are you?"

Billy whirled around and his mouth fell open. He was in a changing room, but it wasn't just any changing room. It was the changing room of the England football team! Billy could see England flags hanging from the ceiling and match strategies on a flip chart in the corner. His eyes nearly

popped out of his head when he saw
messages from all his footballing heroes
stuck to the walls. Then he looked down at
the benches and gasped.

Sitting on a bench, staring up at him, was
a boy who didn't look very much older than
Billy. He was wearing an England shirt with
the number seven on it. He was wearing
white football shorts and very expensive-
looking football boots, and he was rubbing
his ankle.

"You're England's secret weapon!" Billy
said with a gasp.

The boy grimaced.

"Yes, I'm supposed to be," he said. "But I've just tripped over and sprained my ankle. I can't even walk, let alone play football!"

Billy felt a wave of horror crash over him. England's hopes were resting on this boy. Could they win without him?

"I need you to get a message to the coach," said the boy. "Tell him that Birly's sprained his ankle, will you?"

"Birly?" repeated Billy.

The boy turned so that Billy could see the back of his shirt. It said:

BIRLESON
7

"My name's Olly Birleson, but everyone calls me Birly for short," the boy explained. "The plan was for me to go on in the last minute. You have to tell the coach that I can't play!"

"But I don't know the way to the stadium," said Billy.

"That's easy," said Olly. "Out of here, turn right and right again. Then just keep going."

"No problem," said Billy.

He poked his head out into the corridor, checked that no one was coming and then set off. But he hadn't walked very far when he heard a shout behind him. It was the gorilla-like security guard!

"Stop!" yelled the guard.

Billy ran. He just had to get Olly's message to the coach! He scooted to the end of the corridor, turned right into an arched tunnel and sprinted faster than he had

ever gone before. He
could see a bright
light at the end
of the tunnel,
and the cheers
of the crowd
were much, much
louder now. He
was close!

Head down, arms
pumping, Billy shot out of the tunnel and
straight onto the pitch. He didn't notice
the roars of the crowd when they saw him.
He forgot that he was still wearing his
number-seven shirt. He hardly heard them
chanting "Secret weapon! Secret weapon!"
All he cared about was getting away from
the guard. A ball rolled under his feet and
he booted it aside as hard as he could.

"GOOOOAAAALLLL!"

The roar was deafening. It crashed around Billy like a tidal wave. He heard the whistle blow to signal the end of the match. He felt arms go around him and lift him into the air. And then, at last, he understood the wonderful truth.

BILLY HAD SCORED THE WINNING GOAL!

The stadium went wild. The team threw him into the air again and again.

"That's not Birly!" one of them shouted.

"SHHH!" said the goalkeeper. "We don't need to mention that! We WON!"

The next few minutes were a dizzy blur of cheers and hugs and waving to the crowd. The coach grabbed Billy and squeezed him until he thought his bones might crack.

"You're a wonder boy!" he said. "Who are you?"

Billy explained about the

sprained ankle, and the coach hugged him again.

"I'll give you anything you want!" he declared, rather rashly. "Just name it and it's yours!"

Billy thought hard. What did he really want? For months his only wish had been to watch England win the World Cup. And now he, Billy, had actually won it for them. What else could he possibly ask for?

"Erm, could you arrange for the security guards to set my dad and sister free?" he asked. "And could we have season tickets to watch our home team?"

"Of course!" said the coach, feeling relieved that Billy hadn't asked for a mansion with a swimming pool. "But also, I want you to come and collect the trophy for the team."

Fifteen minutes later, Billy was holding the famous golden trophy above his head. He could see Mr Bonkers and Betty jumping up and down in the crowd.

"That's my son!" Mr Bonkers was bawling. "It was me who taught him how to play football! That's my boy!"

"How does it feel to be England's secret weapon?" asked the coach.

A grin stretched across Billy's face. It was the biggest grin that he had ever given. It might even have been the biggest grin in the world.

"Well," said Billy, soaking in the cheers from the stadium all around him, "I guess I just did what I had to!"

THE END

**If you liked
Billy Bonkers,
turn over for more
fantastically
funny stories!**

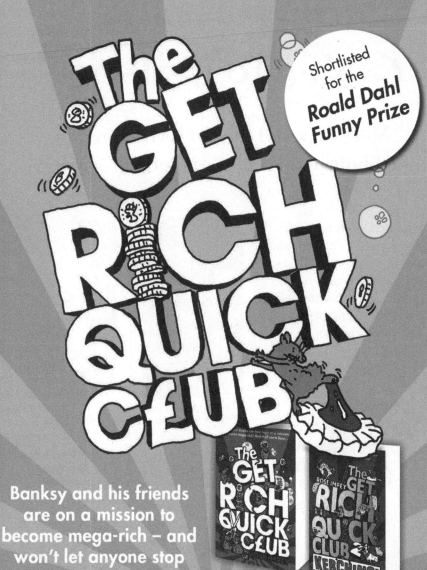

Max and Molly's Guide To Trouble

Meet Max and Molly: terrorising the neighbourhood really extremely politely...

Max and Molly's guides guarantee brilliantly funny mayhem and mischief as we learn how to be a genius, catch a criminal, build an abominable snowman and stop a Viking invasion!

978 1 40830 519 5 £4.99 Pbk
978 1 40831 572 9 eBook

978 1 40830 520 1 £4.99 Pbk
978 1 40831 573 6 eBook

978 1 40830 521 8 £4.99 Pbk
978 1 408 315743 eBook

OUT NOW!

978 1 40830 522 5 £4.99 Pbk
978 1 408 315750 eBook